Sheila
Happy Birthday!
With Much Love

Barb
11/96

Sad
UNDERWEAR
and other complications

Children's Books by Judith Viorst

Sunday Morning
I'll Fix Anthony
Alexander and the Terrible, Horrible,
  No Good, Very Bad Day
My Mama Says There Aren't Any Zombies,
  Ghosts, Vampires, Creatures, Demons,
  Monsters, Fiends, Goblins, or Things
Rosie and Michael
The Tenth Good Thing about Barney
Alexander, Who Used to Be Rich Last Sunday
If I Were in Charge of the World and Other Worries
The Good-Bye Book
Earrings!
The Alphabet from Z to A (With Much Confusion on the Way)
Sad Underwear and Other Complications

sad underwear
and other complications

more poems for children and their parents by
JUDITH VIORST

ILLUSTRATED BY RICHARD HULL

ATHENEUM BOOKS FOR YOUNG READERS

Atheneum Books for Young Readers
An imprint of Simon & Schuster Children's Publishing Division
1230 Avenue of the Americas
New York, New York 10020

The text of this book is set in Souvenir.
The illustrations were done in pen and ink.

Printed in the United States of America

10 9 8 7 6 5 4 3 2 1

Library of Congress Cataloging-in-Publication Data
Viorst, Judith.
       Sad underwear and other complications / by Judith Viorst ;
illustrated by Richard Hull. — 1st ed.
                    p. cm.
       Includes index.
       Summary: a collection of poems that examines a wide variety of feelings
and experiences from a child's point of view.
       ISBN 0-689-31929-0
       1. Humorous poetry, American. 2. Children's poetry, American.
[1. Humorous poetry. 2. American poetry.] I. Hull, Richard, 1945– ill. II. Title.
PS3572.I6S23 1995
811'.—dc20   94-3357

For Kate O'Hanlon

CONTENTS

Sad underwear
and other complications

QUESTIONS

FIRST DAY OF SCHOOL

Will they let me go when I need to go to the bathroom?
And what if I get lost on my way back to class?
And what if all of the other kids are a hundred, a thousand,
    a million times smarter than I am?
And what if we have a spelling test, or a reading test, or
    an . . . anything test, and I'm the only person who doesn't pass?

And what if my teacher decides that she doesn't like me?
And what if all of a sudden a tooth gets loose?
And what if I can't find my lunch, or I step on my lunch, or
    I (oops) drop my lunch down someplace like the toilet?
Will they just let me starve or will somebody lend me a
    sandwich? A cookie? A cracker? An apple? Some juice?

And what if they say, "Do this," and I don't understand them?
And what if there's teams, and nobody picks me to play?
And what if I took off my sneakers, and also my socks, and
    also my jeans and my sweatshirt and T-shirt,
And started the first day of school on the second day?

CREDIT

You asked me to do it.
I promised to do it.
I planned to do it.
I started to do it.
I really meant to do it
Except I forgot.
Couldn't I get some credit
For promising,
Planning,
Starting,
And really meaning to do it?

Guess not.

SAYS WHO?

Who decided that vegetables are something a growing child needs?
Who decided that wonce is spelled o-n-c-e?
Who decided that roses are flowers and dandelions are weeds?
Not me.

Who decided you have to wait till everyone else gets their food,
No matter how starving-to-death you happen to be?
Who decided that, rather than funny, burping is always just rude?
Not me.

Who decided that pussycats are not as important as aunts?
Who decided a person can't live in a tree?
Who decided that jeans don't get counted as dress-up-for-
    grandmother pants?
Not me.

Who decided that birthday days can only come one time a year?
What's wrong with five times a year? Maybe four? Okay, three?
Who decided which things are called normal and which other things
    are called weir-
D? Not me.

RAGGEDY GIRL

There's a raggedy girl in raggedy clothes
With snarly hair and a runny nose
And she lives in a raggedy person's kind of place.
We're both of us about the same size.
We've both got bangs and dark brown eyes.
We've both got freckles polka-dotting our face.
But I go home to cookies and milk,
And a cozy comforter soft as silk,
And she goes where it's scary and sad to be.
Is this an accident? Was it planned?
Can somebody help me understand
Why the raggedy girl should be her,
And I should be me?

WORLD
OF
WONDERS

IT'S A WONDERFUL WORLD, BUT
THEY MADE A FEW MISTAKES

It's a wonderful world, but they made a few mistakes.
Like leaving out unicorns and putting in snakes.
Like no magic carpets, no wishing wells, no genies.
Like good guys getting picked on by the meanies.
Like arithmetic, especially multiplication.
Like expecting a person to stay at home for one whole week with a
    sitter while that person's mother and father take a vacation.
Like needing to finish the green beans to get the dessert.
Like everyone caring *way too much* about dirt.

Like letting there be a cavity in a tooth.
Like calling it a lie when all that this person has done is not
    mention part of the truth.
Like raining on soccer games, and liver for supper.
Like bunk beds where the younger person always gets stuck with the
    lower and the older person always gets the upper.
Like leaving out mermaids and putting in splinters and bee stings
    and wars and tornadoes and stomach aches.

It's a wonderful world, but they made a few mistakes.

MORNING SONG

I sneaked up on the morning
Before the night was done.
The sky had one foot in, one out, of bed.
Upon the sleep-time blackness
The fingers of the sun
Were finger-painting streaks of wake-up red.
Outside my bedroom window
Birds argued in a tree
Was it (chirp) or was it not (chirp) dawn,
Until, as far and wide and high as I could see to see,
I saw the darkness
Going
Going
Gone.

WILL WONDERS NEVER CEASE?

The Seventh Swimming Lesson

Stop the presses.
Call a reporter.
Sally just put her face in the water.

Take That!

Read all about it
In white and black.
Mosquito bit Bonnie
And Bonnie bit back.

We Interrupt This Program

We interrupt this program
To announce that Kevin can
Spell all,
Well, maybe almost all,
Of Af
Or is it Aph
No Af
Afgan
Afganis
Yes! Afghanistan!

HALF MOONSHINE

The moon is the sun's silver mirror.
The moon is a chunk of green cheese.
The moon is the home of the man in the moon.
The moon tugs the tides of the seas.
The moon is where astronauts moon-walked.
A cow once jumped over it too.
Half of these stories are moonshine.
Half of these stories are true.

The moon has astonishing mountains
Piercing the lonely moon sky.
The moon has a goddess—Diana's her name.
The moon is a million miles high.
The moon marks each month as it passes
And has since the world first was new.
Which of these stories are moonshine?
Which of these stories are true?

KNOCK KNOCKS

SAD UNDERWEAR

Knock, knock.
                Who's there?
Someone with sad underwear.
                Sad underwear? How can that be?
When my best friend's mad at me,
Everything is sad.
Even my underwear.

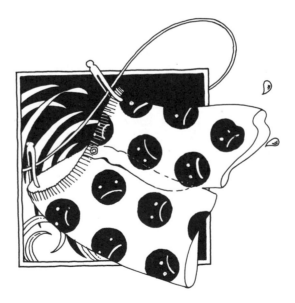

HAIR

Knock, knock.
          Who's there?
Someone with youcrazy hair.
          Youcrazy hair? What does that mean?
When you dye your hair bright green,
Everybody asks,
What are you, crazy?

TRUST ME

Knock, knock.
                Who's there?
The cannibal who lives upstairs.
                A cannibal? Then I'm dead meat.
Nonsense! Do you think I'd eat
My neighbor?
Crunch.
Yum.
Never trust cannibals.

FAIRY TALES

. . . AND BEAUTY AND THE BEAST, ONCE THE SPELL HAD BEEN BROKEN, LIVED HAPPILY (SORT OF HAPPILY) EVER AFTER

It was fun to be the best-looking one in the palace.
It was fun to get all of the compliments and applause.
Yes, I was a pearl among girls
With my milky-white skin and bright curls,
While he was the hairy beast with the snout and the claws.

It was fun to be the best-looking one in the palace.
It was fun—till the spell was broken and he was released
To become a prince so divine
That his gorgeousness far outshone mine.
Now everyone thinks he's the beauty and I'm the beast.

28

. . . AND WHEN THE QUEEN SPOKE RUMPELSTILTSKIN'S NAME, HE BECAME SO ENRAGED THAT HE TORE HIMSELF IN TWO

My father the miller had lied to the king.
He had said I spun straw into gold.
And although I knew not how to do such a thing,
I was locked in the lie he had told.
I was locked in a room with a spinning wheel,
And some straw, and this terrible lie,
And told if I failed to spin straw into gold I would die.

Remember this story? A dwarf cuts a deal:
In exchange for my necklace, my ring,
And my future first baby, he'll sit by the wheel
Spinning straw into gold for the king.
It's not fair to blame me—I wanted to live.
So I did just what you would have done.
I was saved. I was queen. Then the dwarf returned for my son.

You must keep your promises, people will say.
But I had little honor or shame.
For I could not—would not—give my baby away.
And with three days to guess the dwarf's name,
I (cheating a little) discovered his name.
When I spoke it, the creature went wild.
I cared not a fig. I had won. I could keep my first child.

The miller's young daughter is now an old queen,
And I do not sleep well at my age.
There are nights when I dwell on that long-ago scene
Of the dwarf, torn apart by his rage.
Yet when I recall how, afraid and alone,
I was saved by the gold he could spin,
I wonder what I might have done to save Rumpelstiltskin.

. . . AND AFTER A HUNDRED YEARS HAD PASSED, SLEEPING BEAUTY AWOKE (AT LAST!) FROM HER SLUMBER

The drawbridge is creaking.
The castle is leaking.
The royal crown is rusting.
The throne room needs dusting.
Cobwebs hang from my crystal chandeliers.
How can you ask a princess
To deal with this terrible mess?
Wake me again in another hundred years.

. . . AND THE FISHERMAN ASKED FOR NO REWARD FOR SPARING THE LIFE OF THE FISH, BUT THE FISHERMAN'S GREEDY WIFE WAS NOT CONTENT

We lived in a hovel,
A dark dirty hovel.
I was not content.
That magical fish
Owed my husband a wish,
So back to the sea I sent my fisherman husband.

The water had turned from greeny blue to gray.

I wished for a cottage,
A bright pretty cottage.
So off to the sea he went.
I got my cottage,
A most pleasant cottage.
But I was not content.
So back to the sea I sent my fisherman husband.

The water had turned from gray to purple-black.

I wished for a palace,
A grand golden palace.
So off to the sea he went.
I got my palace,
A shimmering palace.
But I was not content.
So back to the sea I sent my fisherman husband.

The water was bitter black and churning, churning.

I wished to be king,
Not a queen but a king.
So off to the sea he went.
I got to be king,
A silver-crowned king.
But I was not content.
So back to the sea I sent my fisherman husband.

The black churning water was roiled by a whipping wind.

I wished to be emperor,
Not king but an emperor.
So off to the sea he went.
I got to be emperor,
An ermine-robed emperor,
But I was not content.
So back to the sea I sent my fisherman husband.

The black churning water, whipped by the wind, crashed against
    the shore.

I wished to be pope,
The high holy pope.
So off to the sea he went.
I got to be pope,
The ruby-ringed pope.
But I was not content.
So off to the sea I sent my fisherman husband.

The wind-whipped water smashed the shore, and the waves rose
    higher and higher.

I wished to be God,
To be just like God.
So off to the sea he went.
Till I was the one
Ruling stars, moon, and sun,
I'd never be content.
So back to the sea I sent my fisherman husband.

The seething water, stirred to a frenzy by the raging storm,
    smashed the shore with waves as tall as mountains, while thunder
    and lightning split the sky, and trees and houses were splintered
    as if they were matchsticks.

We're back in our hovel,
Our dark dirty hovel.
The sea is again greeny blue.
And I'm hoping that fish
Will grant one last wish:
The bright pretty cottage will do.
Yes, the cottage,
And the palace's gold,
And the crown and the ermine robe,
And the ruby-red ring of the pope
Might make me content.
So back to the sea I sent my fisherman husband.

He says he's not going.

. . . AND WHILE POOR HANSEL WAS LOCKED IN THE WITCH'S CAGE, AWAITING HIS DOOM, CLEVER GRETEL CAME TO HER BROTHER'S RESCUE

The witch had dinner reservations.
(My brother was the dinner.)
I was the clever person who made her cancel.
I gave her a shove in
The burning oven.
My brother owes me his life.
So why don't they call this story
"Gretel and Hansel"?

STUFF YOU SHOULD KNOW

RIGHTS AND WRONGS

Manners

Telling a lie is called wrong.
Telling the truth is called right.
Except when telling the truth is called bad manners
    and telling a lie is called polite.

The Hardest Thing

If you think that the hardest thing is saying you're wrong
    when you've been wrong,
I think you should know
That the really hardest thing is, when you've been absolutely
    right,
Not saying nyah nyah nyah, I told you so.

Arithmetic

Two wrongs don't make a right.
So says my teacher, Mr. Brill.
Two wrongs don't make a right, say I.
But maybe four wrongs will.

DON'T THINK

Don't think rivers.
Don't think fountains.
Don't think mountain streams or creeks.
Don't think pools or ponds or oceans.
Don't think lakes and don't think leaks.
Don't think wells or wet or water.
Don't think showers.
Don't think springs.
Don't think moist or damp or rainy.
Don't think hurricanes or things
That drizzle, dribble, drip, drop, flood, or flow,
When there's no bathroom—and you gotta go.

SOMEDAY SOMEONE WILL BET
THAT YOU CAN'T NAME ALL FIFTY STATES

California, Mississippi,
North and South Dakota.
New York, Jersey, Mexico, and
Hampshire. Minnesota.
Vermont, Wisconsin, Oregon,
Connecticut, and Maine.
Hawaii, Georgia, Maryland.
Virginia (West and plain).
Tennessee, Kentucky, Texas,
Illinois, Alaska.
Colorado, Utah, Florida,
Delaware, Nebraska.
The Carolinas (North and South).
Missouri. Idaho.
Plus Alabama, Washington,
And Indiana. O-
Klahoma. Also Iowa,
Arkansas, Montana,
Pennsylvania, Arizona,
And Louisiana.
Ohio, Massachusetts, and
Nevada. Michigan,
Rhode Island, and Wyoming. That
Makes forty-nine. You win
As soon as you say _____.

ITEM OF INFORMATION

Just in case
You were wondering what a disgrace is:
It's, when you're in public,
Scratching in private places.

WELL, SHUT MY MOUTH

A dentist isn't always a mean kind of person,
Even though he squirts your mouth with fizz,
Even though the hand that is jabbing your gum with the
    novocaine needle
Is certainly his.

A dentist isn't always a fierce kind of person,
Even though his drill goes *bzzz-bzzz-bzzz,*
Even though, when he asks, "Do you floss? Do you brush your
    teeth before bedtime?"
You flunk the whole quiz.

A dentist isn't always a guy kind of person.
Lots of dentists also are a Ms.
People you'd never expect to be a dentist turn out to be
    dentists.
My grandmother is.

SEGECREGET LAGANGUAGAGE

I know a secret language
I'd like to share with you.
    Are you ready?
    Here is how it's done:
You take a word and put a "g" sound into every syllable.
    Dgo ygou gget igit?
    Dgon't ygou thgink igit's fgun?

PALS AND PESTS

WAYNE

Nobody's best friends with Wayne.
He's a fellow who clogs up life's drain.
    You're out in a storm where
    There's lightning and thunder.
    He's brought an umbrella
    But won't let you under.
"Just room here for one," he will say as you
    soak in the rain.
Nobody
Nobody
Nobody's best friends with Wayne.

Nobody's glad to see Wayne.
He belongs in a cage with a chain.
    You lend him some money.
    He won't pay it back. You
    Try borrowing money,
    He'll whine and attack. "You
Are trying to take my last nickel away,"
    he'll complain.
Nobody
Nobody
Nobody's glad to see Wayne.

Nobody's wild about Wayne.
In the butt he's a serious pain.
    He's always around till
    There's something needs hauling.
    Then all of a sudden,
    "My mother is calling,"
He'll say, disappearing from sight like a
    superspeed train.
Nobody
Nobody
Nobody's wild about Wayne.

Nobody's cheering for Wayne.
On the carpet of life he's a stain.
    Don't ask for a sip of
    His Coke if you're thirsty.
    He'll say, "Buy your own," and
    Though kicked, clonked, and cursed, he
Will be what he always has been and will always remain:
    The worm in your apple.
    The stone in your shoe.
    The person who gives you intestinal flu.
    The kind of a guy that the FBI ought to detain.
Nobody's cheering for
Nobody's wild about
Nobody's glad to see
Nobody's best friends with
Wayne.

PHYLLIS

You knew me when I didn't know myself
And when I lose myself you find me.
Whenever things get bad
And I forget the good I've had,
You help remind me.

I tell you of my joys. My joys increase.
I tell my sorrows. They diminish.
And when I want to quit
You keep me going, bit by bit,
Until I finish.

Friendship is an art and you have made
The act of friendship your great art form.
I know that I can bear
The biggest chill because you're there
To keep my heart warm.

ROBBY

Robby wants me to write him a poem.
He wants the poem to say
That he's handsome
And strong
And great at martial arts.
He also wants me to mention
That he knows how to stand on his head
And where Saskatchewan is.
(He doesn't want me to mention that he farts.)

JOSHUA

Joshua's laces are never untied.
Joshua's socks never droop.
There's never any soup on his front
When he's done eating his soup.
He looks you straight in the eye when he speaks
(Just like we're told people should).
Oh, isn't he good, mothers say
When they meet Joshua.

Joshua never forgets to say thanks.
Joshua always says please.
You won't see nasty stuff in his nose.
You won't see scabs on his knees.
He cleans his bedroom once every day
(Instead of once every year).
He's good and he's dear, mothers say
When they meet Joshua.

Joshua's shirttails are always tucked in.
Joshua won't spit or shout.
Nor does he use those terrible words
Like—(you go figure them out).
He'll take a bath without being asked
And never has smelly feet.
He's good, dear, and sweet, mothers say
When they meet Joshua.

Joshua always gets A's on his tests.
Joshua never comes late.
He always brings the spoon to his mouth
(Never his mouth to the plate).
He says his prayers and he always shares.
I'm giving you some advice:
If you don't want to spend the rest of your life
Hearing good, dear, sweet, and nice,
You shouldn't ever let your mother meet Joshua.

SEE THE JOLLY FAT BOY

See the jolly fat boy
Filling up his plate,
Bulging at the belly and
A truckload overweight.
We call him blob and buffalo.
We call him tub of lard.
We're sure he doesn't mind because
There's no one who laughs harder than
The fat boy.

See the jolly fat boy
Jiggling as he goes.
Bet it's been at least five years
Since he's last seen his toes.
We tell him that he looks just like
A movie star: King Kong.
We're sure he likes our jokes because
There's no one who laughs longer than
The fat boy.

See the jolly fat boy
When we're not around.
He's not laughing anymore.
He's staring at the ground
With eyes like winter's drearest days,
Like birds whose mama died.
I think we've never seen the boy
Who lives deep down inside—inside
The fat boy.

adventures

EXPLORING

I'll go to the tree-tangled forests and monkey-wild jungles.
I'll study the boa's constrictions, the crocodile's grin.
I'll peer into steaming volcanoes and icicled caverns.
I'll ponder the sea serpent's slither, the shark's slashing fin.
I'll wander the world and beyond it, by foot and by rocket,
To where the sky ends and mysterious rivers begin.
And nothing will scare me, as long as I just have a socket
So I'll always be able to plug my night-light in.

THAT OLD HAUNTED HOUSE

That old haunted house was so creepy, so crawly, so ghastly, so
    ghostly, so gruesome, so skully-and-bony.
That old haunted house gave me nightmares and daymares and
    shudders and shivers and quivers and quavers and quakes.
That old haunted house made my hair stand on end and my heart
    pound-pound-pound and the blood in my veins ice-cold-
    freezing.
That old haunted house gave me goose bumps and throat lumps and
    ch-ch-ch-chattering teeth and the sh-sh-sh-shakes.
That old haunted house made me shriek, made me eeek, made me
    faint, made me scared-to-death scared, made me all-over sweat.
Would I *ever* go back to that old haunted house?
You bet.

TREED

It seemed to make sense at the time.
And so I decided to climb
To the top of the tallest tree in my backyard.
At seventy feet from the ground
I tried to turn back and I found
Up is easy.
Down is very hard.

I'd climbed by the shine of the sun.
But now all the daylight was done.
The sky above me had darkened and mooned and starred.
I clung in the dark to the bark
And the truth came upon me stark.
Up is easy.
Down is very hard.

I guess I'll still be in this tree
When I turn a hundred and three.
Remember to get me a present and a card.
But send them by bird, not by you,
Or else you'll be stuck up here too.
Up is easy.
Down is very
Very
Very
Very
Very
Very
Very
Very
Very
Hard.

THE LAST COWGIRL OF THE WESTERN WORLD

The last cowgirl of the Western world
Buckles her belt,
Pulls up her boots,
Slaps her broad-brimmed Stetson on her head,
Then saddles her swift white stallion
With the black star over each eye
(She calls him Star Eyes),
And gallops into the setting sun,
Across the wide prairies,
Across the deserts and badlands,
Past mesas and buttes,
Through roaring mountain streams,
Singing *tie-yippie-yie-yo yie-yay*
While the tumbleweed twirls,
While the wild wind whips her hair,
Singing *tie-yippie-yie-yo yie-yay*
To the skydiving hawks,
To the wolves howling high on the hills,
Singing *tie-yippie-yie-yo yie-yay*
As she saves the cattle from rustlers,
The settlers from raiders,
The babies from rattlers,
The covered wagons from plunging over cliffs,
Singing *tie-yippie-yie-yo yie-yay,*
Yippie-yie-yo yie-yay,
As she rides the range
Till it's time to ride the school bus.

moms and dads

OUR MOM'S A REAL NICE MOM
BUT SHE CAN'T COOK

Mom's mashed potatoes taste like dirty socks.
Her instant oatmeal tastes like instant box.
    And if she made a pound cake,
    And she dropped it on your foot,
You'd think that it was half a ton of rocks.

Mom's soup could substitute for Elmer's glue.
It's hard to tell her steak from an old shoe.
    And when she brought her chicken
    To the potluck at the Y,
Three people said they'd rather have the flu.

Mom's boss says she deserves a lot of praise.
But not for tuna drowned in mayonnaise.
    And if he ate her salads,
    Which are soggy as a swamp,
We're positive that he'd take back her raise.

Mom's macaroni's mush, and though she tries,
She wrecks all roasts, incinerates french fries.
    And when they give out ribbons
    For Worst Meat Loaf in the World,
We guarantee that she will win first prize.

Mom looks up recipes in every book.
She took some lessons once. They never took.
    She's kind to kids and animals.
    She smiles more than she scolds.
    She reads us books at bedtime.
    Plays Go Fish when we have colds.
    She's good at fixing leaks
    And changing tires on our Olds,
But all her casseroles turn into gook.
Our mom's a real nice mom but she can't cook.

I'M FREAKING! I'M FREAKING!
MY MOM'S GONE ANTIQUING

I'm freaking! I'm freaking!
My mom's gone antiquing.
And guess who she's dragging along?
    She drives to the country and stops
    At these la-dee-da ain't-we-quaint shops
    Full of really dumb desks with roll tops
She could buy for a song.

Somebody rescue me quick!
I'm about to be sick.

I'm freaking! I'm freaking!
My mom's gone antiquing.
I'd rather get cavities filled
    Or have five broken toes and a crutch
    Than be looking at oil lamps (Don't Touch)
    Or this stupid wood chest called a hutch
For which pine trees got killed.

Help! Let me out of here fast!
I don't think I can last.

I'm freaking! I'm freaking!
My mom's gone antiquing.
I tell her enough is enough.
    But she smiles her best pretty-please smiles
    And keeps promising just ten more miles
    Till we reach the next place with more piles
Of this ratty old stuff.

That's me running out of the door.
I can't take any more.

I can't take anymore.
I'm freaking!
I'm freaking!

WHAT DADS DO

Make bookshelves.
Make burgers.
Make money.
Make funny faces that make you laugh.
Scratch your back when you can't reach where it itches.
Lift you up on their shoulders.
Snore when they're sleeping (but say they don't).
Pitch—but not so fast that you can't hit their pitches.

Play tickles with you when you feel like a silly person.
Snuggle up close with you when you feel like a sad one.
Dads explain electricity
And peninsulas
And help you count the stars.

I wish I still had one.

SPECIAL REQUESTS

PRAYER OF THE GOOD GREEN BOY

Before we're all wrecked
By the greenhouse effect
Could you kindly protect us from frying?
Help wetlands endure.
Make the rivers run pure
So the fishes who live there quit dying.

Please clean up the air
And arrange for repair
Where the ozone layer's torn into tatters.
Let coral reefs thrive
And all species survive
Because even the measliest matters.

Un-acid the rain.
Tell polluters: Refrain!
Help the rain forests gain, not grow smaller.
Make the ecosphere sing.
And—oh yes—one more thing.
Could you please make me four inches taller?

I LOVE LOVE LOVE MY BRAND-NEW BABY SISTER

I love love love my brand-new baby sister.
I'd never feed her to a hungry bear.
I'd never (no! no! no!)
Put her outside in the snow
And by mistake forget I put her there.

I'd never want to flush her down the toilet.
I'd never want to drop her on her head.
I'm only asking if
She by mistake fell off a cliff
The next time we could get a dog instead.

WHOOPS!

I'm really really sorry
That I broke that dinner plate,
And spilled that sauce on the tablecloth,
And chipped that cup,
And dropped that glass on the floor.
Excuse me, did I hear you say
That I should please go out and play,
And not help clear the dishes anymore?
I'm really really really sorry.
Sort of.

COULD WE JUST FORGET WE HAD THIS CONVERSATION?

My sneakers are missing.
I put them right there.
I put them right there on the seat of that chair.
I put them right there on the seat of that chair.
They've been taken.
Of course I know what I'm talking about.
They were there on the seat of that chair.
There's no doubt
They were there on that chair.
Positively.
I *am not* mistaken.

I won't look again.
No, I won't look again.
They were there.
Yes, they were.
They were there.
I put them right there.
I *did too*.
On that chair.
On that seat.
What are you laughing at?
What are you pointing at?
What are you trying to say?

What are these sneakers doing on my feet?

THIS LITTLE REQUEST

Now I don't want you thinking I'm fussy.
I don't want to sound like a pest.
And I hope I won't cause any trouble.
But I do have this little request.

I was taking a nap on the carpet
When you came to visit today.
You walked in the door, started talking,
And neglected to note where I lay.

I'm delighted you've dropped by to see me.
I always love having you here.
But before you begin your next sentence,
Could you please take your foot off my ear?

WHEN I GROW UP

WHEN I GROW UP, I'M GOING TO BE A PILOT, OR MAYBE A TV STAR, OR MAYBE A VETERINARIAN OR THE PRESIDENT, OR MAYBE A FISHING-BOAT CAPTAIN OR A DETECTIVE OR A . . .

Why do they keep on saying to me, "What do you want to be when you
    grow up?"
I've tried and I've tried
To figure out what I would like to be when I grow up.
Do I have to decide?
Or could they just let me wait
Until I'm eight?

WHEN I GROW UP, I'M GOING TO BE
A PRACTICALLY PERFECT PERSON

If a puppy wants something to eat, I'll buy food and feed it.
If a child is lost in a mall, I'll help her get found.
If a garden has been forgotten, I'll water and weed it.
If all of the clocks stop their ticking, I'll have them wound.

If a rabbit is caught in a trap, I'll hurry to free it.
If a boy is shivery cold, I'll give him my coat.
If a violin has to be played, I'll fiddle-dee-dee it.
If a princess has to be rescued, I'll swim the moat.

If a David says don't call me Dave, I'll never once Dave him.
If a Sharon says please call me Cher, I'll call her Cher.
If a baby climbs out on a roof, I'll climb up and save him.
If somebody's needing a friend, you'll find me right there.

But if there's a girl who is needing some hugging and kissing,
You'll find me—missing.

WHEN I GROW UP, I'M GOING TO BE A LAWYER

I wished a wish upon a star.
I heard that when you do,
You mustn't tell what you have wished
Or else it won't come true.
They asked my wish.
I wouldn't say.
It didn't come true anyway.
I'll sue.

**WHEN I GROW UP, I'M GOING TO BE
STRONGER, TALLER, SMARTER, BRAVER, FUNNIER,
FASTER, HAIRIER, AND A WHOLE LOT BETTER AT
SOCCER
THAN MY BIG BROTHER**

Except that my brother is always going to be
Three years, six months, and nine days older than me.

LADY, LADY

Lady, lady, in the valley.
Lady, lady, on the hill.
Come and tell me all your stories.
Lady, lady, say you will.

Tell them in the summer, lady.
Tell them when the snow is deep.
Tell them in the morning, lady.
Tell them when I go to sleep.

Tell them serious and silly.
Tell them, lady, small and grand.
You can even tell them scary
If you'll sit and hold my hand.

Tell of things around the corner.
Tell of things across the sea.
Tell of dwarfs and dragons, lady.
Tell of boys and girls like me.

Tell of pigs and princes, lady.
Tell of buses, blimps, and birds.
Make me cry and make me giggle.
Fill my head and heart with words.

Someday I will be a grown-up.
Someday I'll make stories too.
If you'll just be patient, lady,
Someday I'll tell mine to you.

INDEX